Your Anxiety is a Lying Bitch

Corie Nixon

Nembrotha Books
Wayward Writers Press
2026

To survivors, far and wide,
and the Ruby's open mic crew.

Your Anxiety is a Lying Bitch

Hello, High Water

Born with a mouthful
of clouds,
gray matter
sucked from my mouth,
soul swallowed by a well,
blissfully
ignorant of this hell.

I bob,
a buoy flirting
with sea and air.
Dark waves
break
across my face
until I become them,
tendrils of seaweed winding
through red hair.

I bathe in it,
tepid water inching
up my chest,
my breath seized
by hushed anxieties,
galloping across this fitful brain,
a lover I haven't met.

I'm wet,
and like a puddle I keep spreading
ready to soak and slide
into whatever I need to.

Everyone
braces ahead of the storm,
but I'm already a wreck.

The floodwaters come
but I never do.

Summer Solstice

Like a sweaty handshake

the lack of romance
in our sudden parting
stinks of sex and regret,

your awkward goodbye
so rushed,
I won't choke on a word
as empty as love,
reaching into the damp cave
of your chest
hoping to come out
with more than blood
on my fingers.

At what point
in any relationship
do we realize there is no magic,
only the stoic silence
of running out of things to say,
the weak shiver
of an orgasm that wishes
it was never born?

On this,
longest of days,
I long for
a glimpse of your sultry lips
sighing in a gorgeous gasp.

But it's no use. Springtime
is over. And like any other season
you've come and gone
scattering tasteless gifts,
sultry song lyrics,
and a love that will never go deeper
than memorizing the curve of my ass.

Normalized Trauma

I'm that schmuck
who says "this is fine"
while watching
it all burn down.

I come from a long line
of women crushed
by chronic stress
who make decisions
in the here and now.

Tomorrow might be
terrible
so let's just enjoy this

suspended
here indefinitely,
oblivious.

Some overlook the present
in favor of a theoretical future,
compulsively champing
at the bit.

I'm the opposite,
abstaining from hope
for the days ahead.
Distant headlights
haunt me til they
freeze me stiff.

I'm content in this fishbowl
circling a drain
of simple pleasures
without a care in the world.

I can't survive in the wild
but make like I'm piloting my life
as the future unfurls.

Damage stalks
my every waking hour
(which secretly I adore)

I tell myself the story
I need to believe
in order to inhabit
the magic of the moment
in full form.

I am wired to be
on high alert.
An expert eggshell-walker
knows her worth.

I walk the line
between tragic and noble
so effortlessly
you think it's a con.

I keep swimming
not waving but drowning
while you go on.

No Special Hurry

Inventing a way to exist
that's enjoyable
is for the birds
flung across the blazing
burnt-up sky
while we are weighted
here
under the world's
blanket,
snuggled in creature comforts
and fallacies of death.

Everything is burning
but somehow keeps
sprouting anew.
This is the end they say
only
this platitude
echoes through the ages
of non-endings,
the latest horror,
simply a sequel
and a prequel
of what's to come.

The world breaks everyone,
Hemingway said.
but he also said
those that will not break
it kills.

There is some small defiance
In knowing all this
and raising a glass anyway,
tending to plants,
kissing our lovers,
writing poems.

Perhaps it was the absence
of these indulgences
that did Hemingway in,
his mind singed
by the electric shocks
that blotted out
everything
terrible and wonderful,
serving the same sobering pint
of regularity
day after day
until the world won out.

Existing can be enjoyable
and most of us
hunt for pleasure
drunk with love
living in the exhale
of a long sweet drag.

It's dis-
jointing
but somehow us
misfits
cobble together
this humble offering
we call art
because existing
is
unbearable,
regularly so,
which is why
we make music
and sometimes love
and say "look at the moon!"

even as we all secretly crave
the sour, dark well of the world.
Without its deep depravity
what does any of this even mean?
What on earth would we talk about
If we had nothing
to try to forget?

Fawn

The only way out is through
the looking glass into the past
of persist fear,
the curse of my
conception
couched in misery.
In utero
I heard the screams, .
broken bottles of Bud
and mama's
delusional dreams
flowed through me
born to be
a slave to others' needs.

Trauma is a reaction
not a memory.
It is timeless,
visiting us with such ease.

People, please,
I people please
like nobody's business
bearing my inauthenticity
claiming I'm a chameleon
when I don't even recognize me.

Who is she
when she's not fawning
and flirting
hiding behind this wordplay
so elegantly?

Who is she
when she's not
compromising her beliefs?

Something
intangible and irreplaceable
was beaten out of me.

And yet I refuse to leave,
shedding thousands
of fake faces
floating
and gloating
while my heart races

Who is she?
Who is she?
Who is she?

Your Anxiety is a Lying Bitch

Your anxiety is a lying bitch,
told me a bajillion times
you wouldn't survive,
yet here you thrive
like a dandelion
pummeling through concrete,
desperate to breathe,
like a weed who doesn't know
it's a weed,
you stand tall
fragile as a puff ball
giving it your whimsical all
until you are plucked
and scattered,
gliding like nothing else matters
while the world spins
and ends.

Your anxiety is a lying bitch
pushing fear and rage,
a constant onlooker
powered by shame.
She slinks in the echos
of your shadow,
slinging pain.

See, she was your first friend,
succubus, no choice
but to let that bitch in
as if your life depended on it,
because it did.

You learned how to bury .
things deep,
your ever-watchful eyes
roaming
even in sleep
scanning for furious faces
through thick curtains
of smog.
It hangs in the air
putrid and yellow
staining the walls.

Your anxiety is a lying bitch
she works for the cause
running marathons in your mind
of all that's gone wrong
and all that ever will.

Your anxiety is a lying bitch
and though she means well
it's time to send her to hell
with everything else
you can't change.

You are awkward
and full of rage
bursting with emotions
you can't cage.
The present glints before you
like a blade
but you're not scared
because you own this stage.

The Call of the Void

Like an infinitesimal worm,
a tiny voice tunnels
toward consciousness,
courting chaos.

The branches of
a hundred-year-old tree beckon me
to flatten myself against
its massive trunk,
air thick with the aroma
of funeral flowers
dried and pressed
between pages no one reads.

The notion dissolves swiftly,
as quick as I might
swan dive into concrete,
down that bottle of pills,
or accelerate to top speed.

Death ideation fades
like an island disappearing
just as the sky kisses the horizon,
a chalkboard wiped clean.
The magnetic attraction
to imagining
my final fleeting moments
temporarily forgotten until

the void opens its jaws wider,
pulling me in higher
with a long yawn.

Pawns, life moves us along
as the call echos,
endless and effortlessly.
Undulating
within its languid darkness,
The void never rushes;
it just

waits.

The Greatest Show on Earth

A new study disputes
the link between depression
and levels of serotonin in the brain.
I keep hearing the same story;
that depression is the result of a chemical
imbalance. I picture
a wobbly tightrope walker,
deciding depressive episodes
must be the anxiety-ridden fall
into the net below.

Sometimes I cannot see the net
and I'm certain I'm plummeting
to my death, that my inability to achieve
balance will snuff out the flame of my life
before my eyes can adjust
to the darkness.

And yet, each morning
I rise and swallow the same old pills,
the ones meant to make my brain
work whether it wants to or not.
Shiny, orange Effexor and trendy Wellbutrin,
the happy, skinny, sexy pill—
Only I'm not skinny
and happy and sexy are as ephemeral
as the wings of angels.

What if these drugs
are only temporarily taming
a much larger and more threatening beast?
We know too much
about what goes on behind the scenes
to enjoy the spectacle
of pain in the ring below.

But we humans are
obsessed with label-making,
slapping stickers on the surface of everything
like overzealous office assistants
organizing the files of the mind.
So it is easier to take the pills
that merely make life bearable
than to come face to face
with the existential crisis
of our responsibility to stay alive.

Melancholy still visits me,
settling in my lap, a purring cat
drifting off to sleep.

She snuggles close
until it's time for the show.
Gently, I shoo her away
and climb my ladder.
The audience hushes.
Now
it's just me and the rope.

We're All Broken Here

At last, a place where you
belong, unfettered from the expectation of
calm, people dragged away in broad daylight,
deep fakes on top of deep fakes, a giant
error message stamped across the face of a nation we
never were.

Fettered is the physical body of the other, subjected to
grotesque misfortunes while the world watches. They
say
heavy is the head that wears the crown,
insidious and insufferable horrors pouring from the
jester's poisoned mouth. Pretending we

know what's happening provides
little solace. This
myopic regime cannot see the forest for the trees, can
not admit weakness
or defeat even as it brings us to our knees,
pathetic posturing spreads like a disease.

Quitely from safe spaces we whisper;
resist. We count in real time the
steps to genocide,
tempted to trick ourselves into
Uncomplicated bliss.
Violence permeates and punctuates
what remains of the world we know.

Xenophobia rages, a constant undercurrent,
yanking humanity back to the beginning, a broken
record, ground
zero.

Confirmation Bias

I only hear what I want to hear.
I am a conglomerate of others' ears.
Wicked mouths weave lies,
Bouncing off me into flaming skies.
I deny what I deny
enveloped in a circle-jerk of lies.

Tell me, why do you like what you like
and I'll sow on your button eyes.
Being one of us is the prize
A monolith appearing by surprise.
We stand tall and somehow not at all
cogs in the misinformation machine.

I believe what I believe,
facts and evidence can't trick me.
We will burn down all the trees
We will look away as women bleed.

We only see what we are prepared to see.
We gaze into the TV.

How do you know what you believe?

Trumpisms

Tweet tweet little birdie
with the bright orange hair,
hand hovering over your imaginary button
as you address
all the haters and fools out there.

Startlingly en vogue,
you're modern day presidential.
Too bad the white house is a real dump
and sucking the tit of the statue of liberty
Just got pushed from your schedule.

You promised to build a wall
to keep the deplorables out.
You speak in cryptic code:
Covfefe! Bad ratings! Fake news!
Gratuitous exclamation points
and ALL CAPS
punctuate your infantile shouts.

All the world's a shithole
as you so eloquently said,
marching in spirit with the "very fine people"
of Charlottesville,
unintentionally ironic tiki torches raised high
over their freshly shaven heads.

Look at you, grabbing life by the pussy
and draining the swamp
just like you said.
All the world's a stage
and you're the conductor.
Splayed like a nasty woman across the bed.

Here she is, Miss America,
basking in the encore of white supremacy.
By golly, you've really done it:
All hail President Trump,
Grand wizard of the patriarchy.

**The World Will Break Your Heart
(On How Not to Die in America)**

Yesterday, I read an article about
Jahi McMath, a little girl in Oakland
who, in 2013, entered the hospital
for a routine tonsillectomy
and came out "legally dead,"
her heart still beating thanks to the ventilator
pumping oxygen into her blood.
After the surgery, thirteen year-old Jahi
ate a grape popsicle
before she began hemorrhaging
for hours until her heart
stopped. Five years have flown by
during which her brain has instructed her body
to menstruate. Five years
her mother has recorded videos of her responding
to commands, her mother who
cannot even claim her daughter
on her tax returns,
her mother who has had to endure the indignity
of her child being proclaimed a corpse.
I can't stop thinking that this wouldn't have happened
If Jahi was white
if the specter of a black girl suffering
will ever mean anything
to those who can't seem to bear relinquishing
even a little bit of their power.

Even Serena Williams, a world famous athlete,
had to fight for her life
after just having delivered a baby,
her concerns brushed aside
like dust under a rug
as she came dangerously close to dying.

And I can't stop thinking about the man
in Buffalo
who was declared dead
despite the fact that his family protested
for two hours and forty minutes
until the doctor finally noticed
the vein pulsating in his neck
and conceded that he was indeed, still
alive. Two hours
and forty minutes
during which he might have received
life-saving treatment
instead of dying
in front of his family while an entire hospital
full of white coats and pristine scrubs
stood idly by.

Did you know that in America
hospitals perform credit checks
on patients before providing advanced treatment?
That if you are poor or a person of color
or just plain unlucky
your life can slip away in the blink of an eye?

I, for one, am sick of it,
the illusion that this is the greatest country
in the world. There are no opportunities here
for those not predisposed to claim them
and the rich are only getting richer
as they turn the rest of us
against each other,
for their amusement
or their protection,
I'm not sure which;
but maybe it's both
and that's the real problem.
We are a nation of sadists
torturing and killing one another.
That's the thing about power:
Most human beings
are incapable of having it
without losing
their humanity.

Thought-Terminating Cliches

It is what it is. In God's hands
the cookie crumbles into a billion particles of light.

But what are you gonna do?
Such is life.
Look on the bright side,
this isn't your circus.

Boys will be boys, it's just
the way it works. You only live
once,
or less,
but time heals all
wounds in a vacuum.

We're going to hell
in a hand basket made of
microplastics anyway.

Fuck it, we ball.

Fight Flight Fawn Freeze

On which trauma response
do you lean?

Do you sink silently
in quicksand,
surrounded by squelching
swamp sounds

as past and future unbound
and you succumb to reverie?
Crawling in the velvet dark,
trying not to breathe.

Freeze.

I learn to battle with my tongue
voraciously stuffing
my mouth with puns.
I can cut
a man down.
Cut until all the blood runs out.
But I still flinch
when fists come at me
and I still jump
when someone screams.
Every muscle in my body
tightens as I seethe.
I prepare to

fight

but my mind's the enemy.

Pleasantries
flow, plentiful
when I run out of steam,
no longer able to muster
the enthusiasm to flee.
I become
whoever I need to be.
I smile and laugh,
throwing my head back,
cackling over grief.

Fawning

comes
quick as a teenager
and she knows
how to deceive.

I dream
a whole other life,
full of radiant light
and someone to
protect
the child in me.
I tear at my roots,
fashioning together
a pair of makeshift wings.
I dream
I am a bluebird
who's forgotten how to sing.
I dream of not
flinching as I swoop and swing,

I am in
flight
but the fight's still in me.

Ragtime

Believing in boundaries
is hard when you don't know
what they are.
Just the word

boundaries

brings on violent
waves of anxiety
that bankrupt and break me

until reality
rolls out the red carpet of
of doormats
for every Tom, Dick,
and Jane
who comes my way
bearing platitudes
and attitudes
that would of
gotten my young
smart mouth
slapped
with soap.

I hope
you don't
give up now,
reclining into
the abyss
as you seethe
deep inside.

Instead
I hope
you refuse to hide;

and by you,
I mean me,
of course,
timid and shy
hiding behind
a brashness that lies
hoping that
you,
my people,
are actually
mine.

Fearing
I'm a fraud,
an ugly frog
who doesn't belong,
who can't write,or sing,
or croak her way
into the party.

I'm sorry
I can hardly breathe
without lying,
compulsively fawning
and quietly dying

a little on the inside
each time
I allow someone to
stomp on my life while I'm smiling

transfixed
by my own twisted
reflection,
a grimace briefly
dancing
across my face
like a ragtime gal.

*How does this happen
with such regularity.*
I wonder,
and then I remember how.

Tupperware Theory

Whenever you lose a sock in the dryer
it comes back
as a Tupperware lid
that doesn't fit any of your containers.

Can you imagine,
a single blue sock
sucked into a vexing vortex,
tiny particles swirling and
bursting apart
to rearrange themselves,
miraculously, into a square red lid,
plastic and full of anger.

We are what we're made of
but what use is a lid that doesn't fit?

I don't know about you
but my tupperware is in disarray
and I've got the wrong ratio of lids to containers.

Plastic permeates the world
and it's a good thing it's round
because you can never have all four corners.

My life is a series
of miscellaneous
things that don't quite fit.

If you accept the general premise,
sure, no one's got corner on life,
let alone three or four.

We, espousers of this theory
cling to the edge
of an era
of blissful ignorance,
irreverence toward
the preservation of old food.

We can't be compartmentalized,
have no interest
in what's airtight.

Misfits couldn't care less
about keeping things fresh.

Outside the box
I'm a rebel and a relic
wired for self preservation.

This theory all starts with a question:
How's life?

And when you answer,
I am swept away
by theories and queries

precisely because I can tell
the lid's not on tight.

Some People

Some people
are built for love
the way mausoleums are built
for memories,
sacred and somber
but somehow saintly,
monuments erected
to house those
too precious
to rest
under
ground.

Some of us
wear our great big bleeding
hearts
on our sleeves.
And some of you
see that as weakness,
praying on what you assume you can dominate,
your bloodthirsty snout
sniffing for blood.

You smugly insist
not loving
makes you strong
and sophisticated,
your new age ways
of touching
everything
leave you
with nothing

wondering

while I
go on loving,
laying the foundation
for something long lasting
someone like you
can never touch.

Some people
are not even built for liking,

comprised of glittering
glass and daggers,
all pinpoints
puncturing
the illusion of romance,
all reality,
devoid of fantasy
and pleasure
and textures
that inspire bliss
at the slightest touch.

Some people
are not built at all,
fueled by entropy
they delight
in unravelling
life's simple pleasures
yanking on joy
like the spool of a cassette tape
to avoid feeling too much.

What can I say?
I'm old school,
spinning like a record baby
right round
and sadly
you're a square,
an endless voice
droning on,
immoble
so still you might as well be dead.

You don't even know it
when you testify
to how little you love
even
yourself
your perpetual pontificating

proof that
that you can't stand the silence,
your judgemental proclamations
stinking of dread.

Some people know nothing about loving
but some of us
are smart enough to know
that it has never been about knowing,
that the loveliest bits of life
lie in the space between
light and darkness
like a tiny ember
refusing to be snuffed out,
glowing.

Russian Roulette

What am I marveling at?
I wonder, wide-eyed,
caught in your crosshairs
where mercy appears
to have taken a vacation,
leaving me and my whims
to fend for myself,
the metallic crunch
of the blood of the hunt
on the leaves.

Beneath my feet
the ground shakes
as you parade by,
a proud bull in a china shop.

Disappointment lies in wait
getting in line
behind devastation
who consumes me
until every last damn dish
disintegrates
and I forget
how to love
anything.

And yet,
the horizon
is somehow
still captivating,

despite you
barrelling through my life,
which is why
I remind myself
not to go back
to that night
you felt
the call of the wild,
asked me
to cock your gun.

You try to trick me
into thinking I'm the hunter,
but it's more like the fox and the hound.
Friends, you say we are,
but soon enough you'll pull the trigger
and I'll pray
for another round.

The Glory

You say you need to live in purgatory
like suffering is your second job
and dodging decisions is your first.
Being suspended in the space between
means staving off the parts of me
incongruent with your idea of worth.

I don't know how love works
you cavalierly claim
fear quaking beneath your smile.
Everything is fake anyway,
you feebly insist
your voice tinged with denial.

You shrug and proclaim
you give
what you can
as if I am a charity,
ever grateful for your crumbs.
I'm endangered
but you don't see
the beauty in my rarity
the miraculous way
I push air out of my lungs.

You see, I keep breathing
even when I'm down to nothing
but guts and tears strung together,

soon just another of your stories.
You say you are no good at choices
so I'm calling it,
dead to rites,
you can have the glory.

Catch of the Day

All men are the same, she
sneers, a slippery
fish staring sideways through
one glassy, rolling eye.

I don't cringe anymore watching
her bony body convulse,
smacking the ground violently
like a flounder's tail.

Fisherman takes advantage of these
epileptic fits. Foaming
at the mouth she snarls and spits
as he squeezes her slick gills.

Yes, he's reeled her in again,
swigging his beer,
no surprise
buried beneath his weathered beard.

He knew she was down there
swimming in circles, waiting
for his blood worm to wriggle
and squirm.

Daughter, she says
*it's the ugliest thing I've
ever seen*

and I'm sure I know
what she means.
As she whispers
I watch her wet mouth open
and close, straining to make out
her garbled speech.

When he grabs
her by the neck her silver
tail swishes and slaps.
as she begs to be
thrown back.

So he hurls her into the uncaring sea.
She lacks the strength to swim away
and goes belly up,
a cautionary tale,
the slow release of giving up
such a sight to see.

Clarity

It's the calm
of catching your breath
after spectacular sex,
when your heart ceases
leaping
in your chest
and the raging ripples
of orgasm subside
into satisfied sighs,
fingers and toe tips tingling,
your body still singing.

Aloft in a brief moment of zen,
this languid lounging
liquefies me
even though I'm still
buzzing like a honey bee,
or a bird climbing aerials
over the fullest trees.
My lovers lips lick
slowly and quick
every literal and metaphorical
part of me
while I sink below my knees,
convulsively at peace,
unbound by release.

Pocket Dictionary

Wife, Webster says,
is woman joined to man,
stuck like a sluttish Siamese twin
to a suit who moves
freely through the world
unaware of her body dragging
like tin cans behind him.

She makes a pretty jangle
on his wrist,
hangs unnoticeably
in the kitchen,
her voice registering only
as a slow simmer seeping
from the hot stove.

He touches her with potholders,
avoiding the smolder of love,
a married man, yes, husbanding
his libido for later,
other whores to score
in the dark where
spouses do not slip
into the room,
where secrets are born like babies.

The secret is this:
He is free, a solo seagull stealing
a ride from the wind, a good time.
Not arbitrarily welded to The Wife,
old lady, nagging shrew
who once wooed him
into wanting to stand
not next to
but only slightly in front of her,

who promised to have and to hold
(or at least roll her between his fingers
once in a while)
like a smooth, brown pebble
in his pocket.

Gray Rock

I transmute into it,
an inconspicuous
blob of oblong stone.

In my mind's eye,
I am safe,
tucked
in the topsoil
and overgrowth
of a garden scene
so picturesque you might cry.
(I can imagine whatever I like.)

An ordinary slug slides
against my underbelly
to snuggle itself to sleep.
(I pray the Lord my soul to keep.)

There is no chaos here,
only light and air.
(And other rocks with familiar tales.)

If I had lungs
I could actually breathe.

(If I had feelings
I could actually release.)

But I'm just a lumpy,
large pebble
sunning itself
somewhere far from fear.
(I haven't felt this solid
in all my years.)

In human form
I'm in hot water
up to my ears.
(But isn't that why I'm here?)

A gray rock
doesn't have panic attacks,
wonder what it lacks,
it doesn't worry
people might be whispering
it's crazy

(it doesn't feel
anything).

I WANT MY ROCK

The man's deep voice reverberated through the walls
of the shabby duplex. I can still hear his
fist cracking against the door,
knuckles thundering down in quick succession, then,
a final perfunctory thud.

On this late Friday night
the sounds of someone else's misfortune
soothed me.
Despite the addict next door
I could finally sleep.
My family reunited
after another of mother's attempts to flee
from the misery of my father.
Just eleven, I didn't want to have to choose
although I could feel the damage between them
intimately.
Children are always listening.

Some weeks after the "rock" incident the neighbor lady
entered the backyard where I frequently played,
requesting to cut through our little patch of grass.
She slinked through the alley way,
slipping into her bedroom window
to retrieve her things,
mumbling about the bastard landlord
who was kicking her out on her ass.
For weeks candles shined through
her drapeless windows,
no utilities.

That afternoon, a big truck pulled up,
And the strung-out neighbors began loading up
their things,
carrying boxes
late into the night
as we prepared ourselves for sleep.

The next morning I woke up to my dad screaming
THEY HIT OUR CAR!
waking me and my mom, who loved to sleep.
We ran outside and saw my mother's car,
a long white Cutlass Supreme, crumpled
like an empty soda can, folded around a tree.

Parked along the curb the night before,
my parents surmised that their dear neighbor
decided to leave
one hell of a memory.
Using the brunt of a moving van
to smash the car against a dogwood tree.
I wonder, as she did it,
if she thought, if only for a second,
about how much easier it is to assign blame
than to admit that your own demons
are eating you alive.

The surrounding neighbors, of course,
didn't see or hear a peep.
It was the kind of place
where people minded their own business,
safe behind a curtain of unspoken rules.
But the woman didn't get away entirely free,
underestimating the wrath of my mother,
a tiger who locked eyes instantly on her target
one afternoon peeling out
of the Farm Fresh parking lot.

The car was still mangled,
shattered glass spread like crystals across the backseat.
I tried to stop her, begged her to just drive home,
but to no avail. I was invisible,
my voice muzzled by my mother's rage;
a horrific monster I could never unsee.

She tailgated the woman relentlessly,
blowing her horn and screaming
as I slinked down in the passenger seat, praying
to die, fearing after years of beatings
I'd finally see my
mom murdered right in front of me.
She weaved through traffic skillfully until
the woman came to a stop,
pulling far up into the driveway
of her boyfriend's house.

Mom jumped out of the car, screaming
crackwhore, stupid bitch
and various other unpleasantries.
I couldn't take my eyes off of her blood red face
as I began to cry, sinking lower in my seat.
At any moment, I thought, they're going to shoot her,
attack her, call the police.
Time stretched into a limitless void
as I watched the warped scene through my tears
my mom shrieking
that the woman was a lying piece of shit, a druggie.
Finally, mom got back in the car
and every muscle in my body sighed.

We drove home in silence
my mother still fuming as I tried not to breathe.
Back home I shut myself in my roomand collapsed.

That night my mother told my father the story,
buzzing with hate-fueled energy,
oblivious to
her utter disregard for me.
Puffing away on weed and cigarettes, popping pills,
her own addiction a harbinger
she willed herself not to see.

Only now do I recognize her denial as self-hatred
her rage a siren blaring
as she convinced herself she was made
for a life much finer than this.

Resentment is a powerful drug
that steals your identity. After that day,
it replaced my mother:
A hypocrite,
permanently.

First Wedding

I do, I do, I do
I thought
as doom sank deep inside my belly
and settled there
like a stiff drink.

His pale blue eyes
floated aimlessly
in a sea of white,
evoking supremacy,
his shaven blond scalp glinting in the sun.
Doubt flickered beneath my smile
as I recalled our bickering
on the car ride to the courthouse
where the justice of the peace
unceremoniously recited the script
he'd read a thousand times before,
forgetting the rings
and asking me, of all people, to obey.

Breakfast followed at a greasy diner
in a seedy part of town.
I ate pancakes with strawberries on top
and swallowed my orange juice silently
as the morning dragged on. This
wasn't the way it was supposed to be
but I was too proud, too stubborn, and too young.

He did love me, in his way,
though not nearly as much
as he loved himself.
Perhaps if I'd had
even a pinch of his arrogance
this never would have happened.

If only I'd been the narcissist
when he asked me to change
I'd have scoffed in his smug face.
If only I'd known my worth then
I'd have cashed in my chips
before I let him take things from me
that money could never replace.

Auld Lang Syne

You promise yourself
this year will be different
that you will pull yourself out
of the thick black sludge
of your depression
to do the faintly possible
things
your restless body dreams of.

As people all over the world
make their own resolutions
you resolve to be faithful
like the sun
to rise and sink below the horizon
with regularity
to work silently
the way that time works
at the delicate skin around your eyes
folding and unfolding in on itself
effortlessly
In a fine, imperceptible pattern
that only reveals itself
once you back away from it
distancing yourself from the stranger
blinking back at you
who is suddenly
old.

You try to be optimistic
as winter hunkers down in your bones.
They ache,
like the remnants of a bad dream
gnawing at your consciousness
as you lather this unfamiliar body
trying to rinse the vague unpleasantness
from your brain
and between your legs
the full moon tugging at your womb
as the blood begins to flow.
At least something still works
you think
as you head out
into the record breaking cold.
The weatherman on television
frets over his maps
while hurried shoppers
clear the shelves
in anticipation of snow.

You wonder if it will come at all
And if it does, is it a good omen? Or
perhaps a silent rebuke
of your entitlement
sternly chipping away at your ego.

You're ashamed to admit
you think you deserve
a new beginning.
January
doesn't discriminate,
Its brutality is total.
Living things die,
or are frozen in time;
glazed cold.

This year, perhaps,
you will learn to lean in,
to survive the only way
anything feminine
knows how to

by blending into the ice
and steeling yourself
against the season
until spring reluctantly arrives
and thaws you out.

A Euphemism
January 2018

It snowed a foot last night,
and temperatures are expected to remain
below freezing for the next three days.
Tonight, while we dream,
everything will freeze:
Slush on the sidewalks,
bridges, the pipes underneath
this whole damn city, people
and animals unlucky enough
to be abandoned outside.
Last week, in Ohio, a dog was found
frozen solid, mid-bark.
At least thirty deaths are attributed
to this storm, which they are calling
a "bomb cyclone"~
A made-up term for
a historic phenomenon, the first of its kind,
the beginning of the end.
Our inept figurehead proclaims
there's no such thing as global warming,
because of course it's colder along the east
coast than it has ever been before;
and cold and warm, they're not the same
thing, are they? I spend
three quarters of an hour digging my car
out of the snow. I dig until my hands are numb,
until they begin to tingle and burn,
because cold and warm, they're kind of
the same thing, aren't they?

Be Your Own Valentine

You are the only person
you'll be stuck with
for the rest of your life.
And it might not be
unbearable
if you'd just unclench your jaw
and welcome the hysterical
free flow of tears
streaming like
leaping off your face
is going out of style.

Did you know
your shadow sticks to you
even in the absence of light?
Some might say
light is what defines a shadow
what conjures it up
but shadows
and darkness
are synonymous
aren't they?

I'm asking you
dear audience
because I cannot
clearly see myself
nor this room
only shadows
dancing across the stage
only nighttime
and the dark moon.

You cannot heal the world
if you cannot heal yourself.
Self-care is self preservation.
Motivation requires the discipline
to drag one's self along
through the muck
of major depression.
How can someone like me
dare to hope,
during these desperate times?

Out to Sea

You are analytic,
sharp,
lover of life
cutting the air
with beams of light,
your lasers slightly
unhinged.

There is a tinge
of fall in the air,
you binge
what makes you
feel like a man,
you know you'll win
and you can.

Your ambition is contagious,
sometimes outrageous
and I am terrified,
deep anchors of pain
embedded in me.

You don't understand,
before your unusual plans
I never dared to dream.

Humblebrag

You're so vain,
you probably think this poem's about you.
And although it might be
it's also about me, how badly
I want to crash my life
like a meteor
but somehow
find the strength
to hurl myself away
into the space between the stars.
We've come too far.
I've stared deep into the sun
yet find myself
drowning in the dark.
I want your heart.

It isn't mine and never will be
which makes me
choke on my own ego.
I have nothing to show
for the years I've wasted,
the time spent drifting along
in someone else's story.
I made a choice
but it was the wrong one.

I didn't know what I was giving up
because it always takes me too long to believe
even though I know
people always tell you
who they really are. I was
such a good student
but somehow
I wasn't paying attention.
This affliction
drains me.

I show you the broken pieces of myself
praying to find a home
in the endless beauty of your eyes.
I cry at how alive I feel
at the simple pleasure of being seen
for the first time
in a long time.

I've been guarding my heart so long
I've forgotten what it feels like
to set it free.
I've said it before:
Your unnerving stare
slays me.

It's a delicious way to be destroyed.
A reckless moth,
I flutter around you
unable to resist
although I know I shouldn't touch.
I want to be a part of your beauty
but fear I am asking too much.

You're so vain
I can't stop writing
poems about you.

I'm so vain
I can't stop hoping
you'll hold me down
and ravish me,
satisfy the wetness between my thighs.
I want your tongue lips teeth hair hands
all over me;
to cry out in ecstacy
at these violent delights.
I don't want a choice
anymore, just your control.
Please
pin me down
until all the wildness within me
comes out
to swallow you whole.

I promise until the day I die
there's nothing you can tell me
that will make me look away.
In my heart of hearts I know
why I have to have you.

It's because we're the same.

Anatomical Secret

Your beauty stretches like a scar
from here to nowhere, a violet bruise
spreading across a surface it cannot mar.
They say that people come in twos,

It's true, footprints on the beach
are never lonely, not like our hearts
that roam the blistering desert and weep.
This barren place is where its starts,

the elegy of love's lies
weaves its tendrils through your hair.
Scavenger, I feed on parts of you that die.
Love, like your white throat, is best seen bare,

your naked larynx jumping as I come near,
whispering *the heart is red, but the soul is clear.*

For all the girls you loved before

who you never loved
more than your own reflection
or their admiration of you.
Do you know what it feels like
to be reduced
to the very thing you are least proud of?
Enshrined in an anecdote you will never escape,
perpetually bent over a tombstone
or detoxing in a dark room,
glittering in the distant past like a groupie
famous for fucking
herself
over and over
by continuing to let you seep into her life.

You are a stain
that won't come out
despite the substances I use to scrub my mind
you've inscribed me.
Everyone knows
I'm an idiot,
a Shakespearian fool who spent her days
entertaining you,
indulging your wayward whims
while you and your hedonism
hunkered down
in my bones.

How do I let go
of something I never had
when I'm still mourning
the things I let you take from me?
I should have iced you out
before you discovered
I was such a willing audience,
in your words,
so accommodating.

You still won't admit it
but I know you know
I'm little more than a projection screen.
I exist to highlight
the best of who you are
but like all the other girls
I seem to have exhausted my usefulness,
just another dumb machine.

Tidal

I can't deny it:
The wet shine in your dark eyes
drags me in
like the jagged edge of an ocean.
Stripped down to sand and bones
my soul reaches for pieces of you,
singing bits of broken glass
and the seductive curve of seashells.
Elusive, you hide from the mapmaker's
prying eye, existing apart from the strain
of lines, a beach with no name.

This is the secret hiding place,
graced by the contours of your face,
the gateway onto a page we've made
from scraps of spirit and song.
Carried here by the salty sea breeze
like any other murmur of a dream
I'm wondering if we felt this coming
all along, the slick grip of seaweed
winding its way into our weathered
hearts.

Over the years I find you here, maybe
the one who saves me from slipping
into the grooves of the wrong life.
Simple as sunrises, something in me moves
as we perform these acts of gentle kindness,
looking for little more than whispers,
wishes, and daffodils in return.
I just want to chase you through a field
of flowers, taste the dripping of the hours,
trace my tongue over the honey
coursing through your veins.

We both fight it, but even the stars
set against the blackness
can see us stumbling toward something,
each step assuring
we'll never be the same.

Hush

It's time for me to shut up,
to wait for you to take my clothes off;
to step back and allow the future to destroy us;
to lose ourselves in stolen glances; keep it hush-hush.

I wait for you. Take my clothes off,
I beg of you darling. Let's
lose ourselves. Stolen glances keep it hush-hush,
but my hands betray my heart, soaring like a starling.

I beg of you, darling, let's
run away and live among the stars; hold
hands. Betray my heart, soaring like a starling,
and I will continue to cling to you like mold.

Run away. Live among the stars. Hold
my gaze with your mossy, muddled eyes.
I will continue to cling to you like mold
writhing like a snake beneath you to stifle my cries.

Your mossy, muddled eyes
tear down every wall I've built. I am helpless,
writhing. Beneath you I try to stifle my cries
of ecstasy, pleasure all wound up with pain as we

tear down every wall I've built. I am helpless,
lost without you, waiting for the future to destroy us.
You are pure ecstasy, pleasure wound up with pain:
it's time for me to shut up.

Winter Solstice

The day folds in on itself
collapsing quietly
like a sandcastle
eroded by a wave.

It's subtle
the way winter waltzes in
like a fever breaking
or a headache subsiding
I hardly notice
that things are dying
immersed in the golden splendor
of the last gasp of autumn.

A chill begins to settle
in my bones
and yet I hold on
to the little bit of warmth I have left
for the year that has both wrecked me
and resurrected me.
Reanimated, I go through the motions,
mocked by muscle memories
that move me
at the mercy of some cosmic
puppeteer.

The past beckons
like a deadly beacon
as I bundle up,
oddly soothed
by the darkness
drawing near.

There is beauty in finality
even the death of the love
I thought I could coax
into survival.
Its demise makes room
for the birth of something new,
the equinox announcing
the reaper's arrival.

Winter preserves
what is dear to me
even if it also means
hardening what was once
lovely
into ice.

The days are shrinking now
like cellophane
and I can't hold on to the light.

A Jug of Water

Motherhood is a jug of water
you lug around everywhere you go.
Some of us bedazzle the jug,
some overflow it,
and some try to shrink it down,
compartmentalizing
or hiding
the mom part of themselves
hoping the cracks
and stretch marks don't show.

Motherhood is a jug of water
my friend Jen says,
You have to keep refilling it,
replenishing yourself
over and over
even when the desert mocks you.
Jen is an athlete,
and a survivor.
She knows something about
digging deep,
reaching and stretching
and scraping
the bottom of the well.

My mother
didn't like water
or the weight of the jug.
I had to find my own
rivers
and bends
and the willpower
to even dream
of picking up that jug
my teenage self
swore I would never carry.

Motherhood is a jug of water
and your babies aren't the only ones
trying to drink it.
The world works us all over
saying *care for me,*
nurture me,
give every last bit of yourself over
and forget who and what you were
before.

That's why
we have to keep refilling the jug
and clamping the lid on tight.
Motherhood is a jug of water
but it is also
sometimes
an empty container,
a gaping wound,
a crack in a tiny Russian nesting doll.

Motherhood is a bucket
collecting raindrops
and soil sucking up water
and a vessel for the world's tears.
Motherhood
is swimming
in an ocean of fear
while desperately trying
to pry the lid
from the jug.

Your Anxiety is a Lying Bitch
2026 Corie Nixon
Nembrotha Books
an imprint of
Wayward Writers Press
waywardwriters.com
Set in Della Resipira and Georgia
Cover Design by Daddy Sir Concert and Band Posters

Corie Nixon has been writing and performing poetry for the last twenty-five years, beginning with performances at open mics in the Hampton Roads area of Virginia in the early 2000s. Her work focuses on the effects of trauma, both singular and collective, and the power of resistance. Corie works professionally with individuals with intellectual and developmental disabilities and has an MA in Gender Studies from ASU. She and her family call the Shenandoah Valley home.